Praise for Nan McCarthy's
CHAT

"Draws you in from page to page. . . . Sequels are on the way, and I can hardly wait."

—L. R. Shannon, *The New York Times*

"By clever combinations of e-mail, live chat, emoticons, and computer shortcuts, she gives the headstrong-girl-meets-self-sufficient-boy story a refreshing twist."

—*Publishers Weekly*

"Could it be a high-tech version of *The Bridges of Madison County?* . . . CHAT is a hip look at the Internet cyberculture and how it has changed the dynamic of present-day relationships."

—Tina Velgos, *The Review Zone*

"Takes a surprising, satisfying turn in a cliff-hanger climax. . . ."
—Sam Jemielity, *New City* (Chicago)

"Nan McCarthy's CHAT deserves a prize for capturing the oddly personal feeling that e-mail communication between two strangers can arouse."
—Pierre Bourque, *The Ottawa Xpress*

"Serve[s] as a primer on how (and how not) to conduct a love affair online. But you won't need a modem to appreciate the charm of this virtual romance. . . ."
—Sara Nelson, *Glamour*

"This may be Silicon Valley's *Story of O.* McCarthy cleverly pulls off a wicked, *Vox*-like trick by making the reader feel like an online voyeur, secretly reading other people's private mail. From the first line, we're hooked."
—Derek Pell, *House Organ: A Magazine of the Arts*

"CHAT says much about the direction of interpersonal and romantic relationships in the digital age. . . . What is most impressive about CHAT is the natural development of the characters' relationship. The author demonstrates a command of how life online really progresses."

—Chris LaMorte, *Westword*

"CHAT is a great little novel. . . . Obviously written by someone who knows the publishing business. . . . While not a romance, the growing familiarity of and intimacy among the clever quips give the book its endearing quality."

—Caren Eliezer, *The Seybold Report on Publishing*

Also by Nan McCarthy

CHAT
CONNECT

Available from POCKET BOOKS

For orders other than by individual consumers, Pocket Books grants a discount on the purchase of **10 or more** copies of single titles for special markets or premium use. For further details, please write to the Vice-President of Special Markets, Pocket Books, 1633 Broadway, New York, NY 10019-6785, 8th Floor.

For information on how individual consumers can place orders, please write to Mail Order Department, Simon & Schuster Inc., 200 Old Tappan Road, Old Tappan, NJ 07675.

CRASH

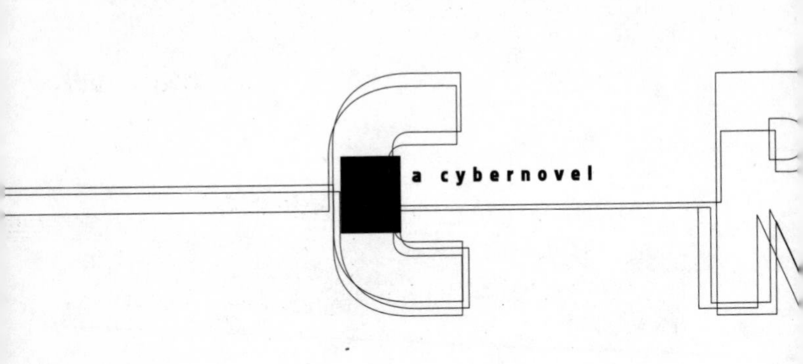
a cybernovel

NAN McCARTHY

POCKET BOOKS
New York London Toronto Sydney Tokyo Singapore

An *Original* Publication of POCKET BOOKS

POCKET BOOKS, a division of Simon & Schuster Inc.
1230 Avenue of the Americas, New York, NY 10020

ISBN: 0-671-02341-1

First Pocket Books trade paperback printing October 1998

10 9 8 7 6 5 4 3 2 1

Cover design and illustration by Blacksheep
Interior design by David J. High

Printed in the U.S.A.

FOR COLEMAN

acknowledgments

This trilogy of cybernovels has come a long way since I wrote and self-published the first book in the series nearly three years ago. Two people in particular have played a key role in helping me fulfill my dreams for CHAT, CONNECT, and CRASH: my agent, Jane Dystel, of Jane Dystel Literary Management, and Greer Kessel, my editor at Pocket Books. Thank you for believing in my work, for your enthusiasm, and for sharing your enthusiasm with others.

In writing this third book in the trilogy, many wonderful people continued to offer me their unselfish support: aviation expert Doug Goldberg, for his advice on e-mail and airplanes; designer and illustrator Eric Lewallen, for his careful and caring work on my Web site; my attorney Steve Collins, for his legal advice and friendship; Miriam Goderich of Jane Dystel Literary Management for her expert advice and friendly support; my fellow writers Marsha Skrypuch, Linnea Dayton, Kathleen Taylor, and Anne Fisher, for their warmth and encouragement; my friend and neighbor Gail McCoy, for her feedback at a critical point in the editing of this manuscript; and my mother, for being my number-one fan. Most of all, I'm thankful to my husband, Patrick, and our sons, Ben and Coleman, for their faith in me as a writer, wife, and mother.

And finally, I am deeply grateful to the many readers of the first two books in this series who sent me e-mails and letters telling me what they thought about my books. I treasure these reader comments.

—Nan McCarthy, October 1997

"It is easier to resist at the beginning than at the end."
—Leonardo da Vinci, *The Notebooks*

preface

If you haven't had the experience of logging on to the Internet or to a commercial online service, or even if you don't yet own a computer, you can still ease yourself into the new terminology of electronic correspondence by glancing through the brief glossary of abbreviations, acronyms, and emoticons at the back of this book. These shorthand words and symbols help people who are communicating via e-mail to inject emotion, tone, and even action into a medium that would otherwise be devoid of the valuable signals we often pick up when listening to a person's voice on the telephone or observing facial expressions and body language when talking in person.

So feel free to familiarize yourself with these online terms by looking at the glossary before you start reading CRASH. Or, you can just dive right in, and refer to the glossary after you've joined Bev and Max on their wild ride through cyberspace.

—Nan McCarthy

CRASH

member profile

Member Name: Beverly J.
ID: BevJ@frederic_gerard.com
Location: Midwest
Birth date: October 11
Sex: Female
Marital Status: Married
Computers: Mac Quadra and a PowerBook
Interests: Reading, playing the piano, studying typography
Occupation: Editor
Quote: *Great works are performed not by strength but by perseverance.*

—Samuel Johnson

member profile

Member Name: Maximilian M.
ID: Maximilian@miller&morris.com
Location: Northern Hemisphere
Birth date: Taurus
Sex: male
Marital Status: single
Computers: who cares
Interests: bonsai gardening, writing poetry, mixing the perfect martini
Occupation: copywriter
Quote: *For myself I live, live intensely and am fed by life, and my value, whatever it be, is in my own kind of expression of that.*

—Henry James

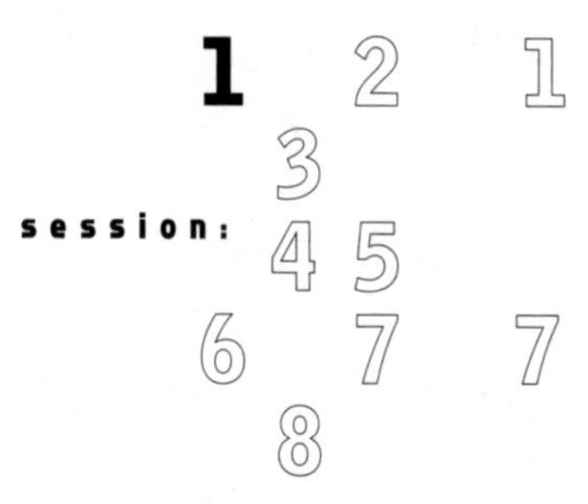

>Private Mail
> Date: Sunday, August 11, 1996 11:27 p.m.
> From: Maximilian@miller&morris.com
> Subj: Wow.
> To: BevJ@frederic_gerard.com

Beverly,

Tonight, I'm the happiest man in the world.

I know you're flying back to Chicago now and that you won't get this message until tomorrow, and that things will probably be pretty hectic for you at work Monday morning, having just come back from your trip and all.

But I wanted to tell you how happy you've made me.

Good night, my love.

Max

> Private Mail
> Date: Monday, August 12, 1996 9:09 a.m.
> From: BevJ@frederic_gerard.com
> Subj: Wow.
> To: Maximilian@miller&morris.com

Max,

My desk is piled high with manuscripts to review; my in box is overflowing with memos, reports, faxes, and other junk; I've got a million phone calls and e-mails to return; and all I can think about is you.

(And your body.)

Bev

> Private Mail
> Date: Monday, August 12, 1996 8:22 p.m.
> From: Maximilian@miller&morris.com
> Subj: Thank you
> To: BevJ@frederic_gerard.com

I keep wondering what I did to deserve you and the weekend we just spent together.

> Private Mail
> Date: Tuesday, August 13, 1996 7:57 a.m.
> From: BevJ@frederic_gerard.com
> Subj: No—thank *you*
> To: Maximilian@miller&morris.com

I don't know, but it must have been something awfully good. <g>

Seriously, Max. I don't think *I* deserve *you*. You're too good for me. And to me.

> Private Mail
> Date: Tuesday, August 13, 1996 2:46 p.m.
> From: Maximilian@miller&morris.com
> Subj: No—thank *you*
> To: BevJ@frederic_gerard.com

Don't say that, Bev. You're a goddess. I worship you. I could never be too good for you.

I've been reliving this past weekend in my mind. I want to talk about it with you but I'm afraid if I start I'll never stop.

> Private Mail
> Date: Wednesday, August 14, 1996 8:18 a.m.
> From: BevJ@frederic_gerard.com
> Subj: Please. Don't. Stop.
> To: Maximilian@miller&morris.com

Hmmm, you mean kind of like this weekend?

Bev

> Private Mail
> Date: Wednesday, August 14, 1996 3:29 p.m.
> From: Maximilian@miller&morris.com
> Subj: Please. Don't. Stop.
> To: BevJ@frederic_gerard.com

What do you mean—kind of like this weekend?

Max

> Private Mail
> Date: Thursday, August 15, 1996 8:16 a.m.
> From: BevJ@frederic_gerard.com
> Subj: Please. Don't. Stop.
> To: Maximilian@miller&morris.com

Being afraid that once we get started we won't be able to stop.

> Private Mail
> Date: Thursday, August 15, 1996 10:56 a.m.
> From: Maximilian@miller&morris.com
> Subj: Please. Don't. Stop.
> To: BevJ@frederic_gerard.com

Ohhhh. I get it. Yes, that was a bit of a problem, wasn't it?

<sheepish grin>

Max

> Private Mail
> Date: Thursday, August 15, 1996 4:59 p.m.
> From: BevJ@frederic_gerard.com
> Subj: Please. Don't. Stop.
> To: Maximilian@miller&morris.com

Problem? You think not being able to stop doing what we were doing is a PROBLEM? As far as

I'm concerned, Max, it was one of the best things about the weekend.

<weg>

> Private Mail
> Date: Thursday, August 15, 1996 9:20 p.m.
> From: Maximilian@miller&morris.com
> Subj: Please. Don't. Stop.
> To: BevJ@frederic_gerard.com

Which reminds me, young lady. Since you missed half of the Macworld convention, what are you going to tell your boss? I mean, isn't he going to wonder why you hardly saw the light of day on Saturday and Sunday, the last two days of the show?

I'm really sorry for making you miss some of your appointments, Bev.

::: eyes cast downward, dolefully kicking toe in dirt :::

Love,

Max

> Private Mail
> Date: Friday, August 16, 1996 7:02 a.m.
> From: BevJ@frederic_gerard.com
> Subj: Please. Don't. Stop.
> To: Maximilian@miller&morris.com

Oh, yeah. You sound *real* contrite, Max. <g>

Don't be sorry. I saw enough of the show on Thursday and Friday, before you came Friday night.

xoxo,

Bev

> Private Mail
> Date: Friday, August 16, 1996 11:52 a.m.
> From: Maximilian@miller&morris.com
> Subj: Please. Don't. Stop.
> To: BevJ@frederic_gerard.com

You mean before I *arrived* Friday night, Your Editorness?

> Private Mail
> Date: Friday, August 16, 1996 5:12 p.m.
> From: BevJ@frederic_gerard.com
> Subj: Please. Don't. Stop.
> To: Maximilian@miller&morris.com

No, I meant what I said: I saw enough of the show before you *came* Friday night.

Bev

> Private Mail
> Date: Friday, August 16, 1996 7:23 p.m.
> From: Maximilian@miller&morris.com
> Subj: Please. Don't. Stop.
> To: BevJ@frederic_gerard.com

Oh. I see. Which time Friday night were you talking about then?

> Private Mail
> Date: Saturday, August 17, 1996 10:10 a.m.
> From: BevJ@frederic_gerard.com
> Subj: Please. Don't. Stop.
> To: Maximilian@miller&morris.com

}:-)

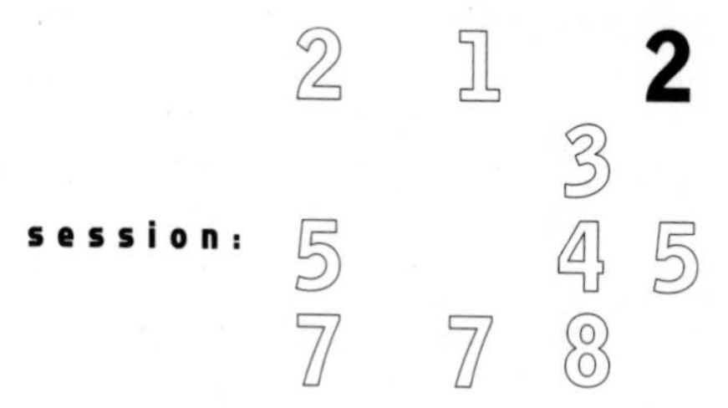

> Private Mail
> Date: Saturday, August 17, 1996 6:17 p.m.
> From: Maximilian@miller&morris.com
> Subj: If
> To: BevJ@frederic_gerard.com

Beverly,

If you were a car
I'd drive you
If you were a plane
I'd fly you
If you were an olive

I'd eat you
If you were a martini
I'd drink you
If you were a song
I'd sing you
If you were a poem
I'd write you
But you're Beverly
so I'll love you

Max.

> Private Mail
> Date: Sunday, August 18, 1996 11:43 a.m.
> From: BevJ@frederic_gerard.com
> Subj: You're a poet & you know it
> To: Maximilian@miller&morris.com

Max,

Thank you for the poem. I loved it. I wish I could write one for you, but I'm not very good at writing poetry.

How can I return the favor?

Bev

> Private Mail
> Date: Sunday, August 18, 1996 1:08 p.m.
> From: Maximilian@miller&morris.com
> Subj: I'm a poet & don't I know it
> To: BevJ@frederic_gerard.com

Bev,

Maybe you could try to write a poem for me someday.

Max

> Private Mail
> Date: Monday, August 19, 1996 6:02 a.m.
> From: BevJ@frederic_gerard.com
> Subj: I'm not a poet & I definitely know it
> To: Maximilian@miller&morris.com

I don't know, Max. I'm good at a lot of things but writing poetry ain't one of 'em.

How else can I entertain you?

Bev

> Private Mail
> Date: Monday, August 19, 1996 9:14 a.m.
> From: Maximilian@miller&morris.com
> Subj: Talk to me
> To: BevJ@frederic_gerard.com

Talk to me about the weekend we spent together.

> Private Mail
> Date: Monday, August 19, 1996 11:18 a.m.
> From: BevJ@frederic_gerard.com
> Subj: Let me...entertain you
> To: Maximilian@miller&morris.com

Okay...but I feel kinda funny doing it when I'm here at work.

Let me think about it a little bit and write a message to you from home.

Bev

> Private Mail
> Date: Monday, August 19, 1996 3:29 p.m.
> From: Maximilian@miller&morris.com
> Subj: Let me...entertain you
> To: BevJ@frederic_gerard.com

Beverly—

I'll be waiting with baited breath.

Max

> Private Mail
> Date: Tuesday, August 20, 1996 8:16 a.m.
> From: BevJ@frederic_gerard.com
> Subj: Let me...entertain you
> To: Maximilian@miller&morris.com

Max,

You mean bated breath.

Bev

> Private Mail
> Date: Tuesday, August 20, 1996 9:21 a.m.
> From: Maximilian@miller&morris.com
> Subj: Huh?
> To: BevJ@frederic_gerard.com

That's what I said.

> Private Mail
> Date: Tuesday, August 20, 1996 11:48 a.m.
> From: BevJ@frederic_gerard.com
> Subj: Huh?
> To: Maximilian@miller&morris.com

No, you said you would be waiting with *baited* breath, and I think you meant that you'll be waiting with *bated* breath.

Unless you have worms in your mouth or something.

> Private Mail
> Date: Tuesday, August 20, 1996 2:38 p.m.
> From: Maximilian@miller&morris.com
> Subj: worms, worms, I'm gonna eat some worms
> To: BevJ@frederic_gerard.com

Beverly, sometimes you annoy the hell out of me.

Love,

Max

p.s. Do you always go around correcting people's grammar and spelling? Some people might not find that amusing, you know.

> Private Mail
> Date: Wednesday, August 21, 1996 7:58 a.m.
> From: BevJ@frederic_gerard.com
> Subj: Nobody likes me everybody hates me
> To: Maximilian@miller&morris.com

And here I was the one who was always saying how *you* annoyed the hell out of *me*. Looks like the tables have finally turned. <g>

xoxo,

Bev

p.s. Yes, I'm a compulsive member of the grammar and spelling police. I try to refrain from correcting people at cocktail parties, but I don't always succeed. Trying not to edit restaurant menus is enough to make me crazy.

> Private Mail
> Date: Wednesday, August 21, 1996 10:02 a.m.
> From: Maximilian@miller&morris.com
> Subj: Everybody loves somebody
> To: BevJ@frederic_gerard.com

Well I still find you amusing. And you even got me to look up "bated" in my dictionary.

I'm learning a lot from you.

Max.

> Private Mail
> Date: Thursday, August 22, 1996 6:22 a.m.
> From: BevJ@frederic_gerard.com
> Subj: sometime.
> To: Maximilian@miller&morris.com

And I you.

Bev

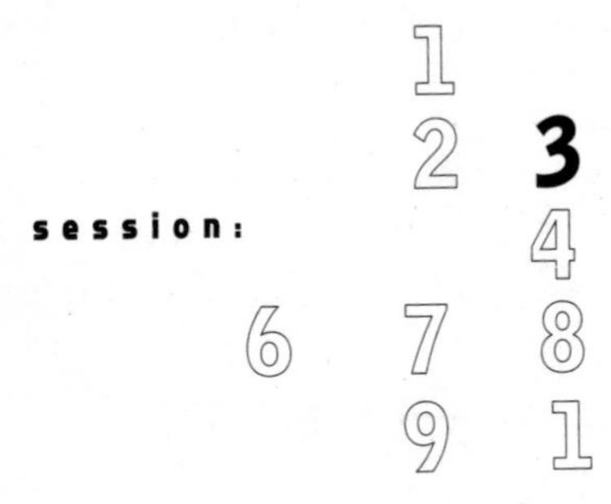

> Private Mail
> Date: Friday, August 23, 1996 8:09 p.m.
> From: BevJ@frederic_gerard.com
> Subj: Lovin' Spoonful
> To: Maximilian@miller&morris.com

I was a nervous wreck while waiting for you to arrive at my hotel that Friday night. I had received your phone message earlier in the day saying you would meet me in the lobby at 7:30, so at least I knew what time you would arrive.

After I got back from the show that day I took another shower so I could wash the hairspray out of my hair and put on fresh makeup and clothes. And new underwear.

It was a good thing I brought so many different outfits with me. Even Gary wondered why I was bringing such a huge suitcase for just a four-day trip. I spent 45 minutes trying on various outfits for you. I wasn't sure if I should wear an evening dress or one of the suits like the one you first saw me in. Or maybe I should go with something casual instead, jeans and a summer knit top, so I wouldn't look like I was making too big of a deal out of seeing you again.

I stood in front of the mirror in my room and thought about which of the clothes would be easiest for you to take off, because this time, instead of taking off my clothes in the bathroom, I wanted you to undress me. And I knew that's what you would want, too. I decided to wear a skirt with a silk blouse.

When you walked into the lobby I couldn't believe how stunning you looked. You were more handsome than I remembered, even more so than

I had been imagining in all the months we were apart. And I was glad you left your overnight bag in the trunk of your car, because I don't think I could have stood the awkwardness of bringing your stuff up to my room and then coming back downstairs for dinner. I wanted us to be able to stare at each other across the dinner table for several hours, savoring the chemistry, before we devoured each other upstairs.

You're so easy to talk with, Max. I wish I had your gift of gab. I can see why everyone likes you. I've never had much patience for small talk, but you make everything seem important and entertaining, even the most trivial things. You made everything that night seem so effortless.

I wanted to order something light like the Caesar salad so I wouldn't be too full when we finally went upstairs, but I knew you would haze me for that so I ordered the type of thing I would normally order: stuffed pork chops with steamed vegetables and mashed potatoes. (So now you know that I, too, have a big appetite.) I wasn't surprised when you ordered the 17-oz. sirloin and a baked potato. I especially enjoyed watching you spend several minutes telling the waitress how you wanted your martini (very dry—just wave the bottle of vermouth somewhere in the vicinity of the glass—make sure the glass is chilled, and don't forget the anchovy olives). I was touched when you asked the waitress on my behalf what sort of beer they had, and pleased to learn they still carried one of my favorites, Lienenkugel Berry Weis. (A berry good beer!)

I was glad each of us didn't have more than two drinks with dinner, because I wanted us to be relaxed but not too tipsy. I was also glad that you didn't seem to be in any hurry for the dinner to be over, because I was still a little nervous even though you did everything you could to make me feel at ease.

Three hours later, by the time we shared a piece of cheesecake and a big glass of ice water, I wanted to lunge across the table and rip your clothes off and smash myself against you. My insides were hot wax.

I liked the fact that you didn't ask me if it would be all right if we went straight up to my room after dinner or what I wanted to do or anything like that. Once we asked for the check it was pretty much understood what was going to happen next and there really was no need for discussion. I liked staring at you in the elevator in silence and I liked you staring at me.

What happened after that were some of the most powerful moments of my life. I couldn't believe how fast everything happened from the moment I inserted the credit card key in the lock and heard the latch on the door click as it turned beneath my hand. For the rest of the weekend every time I heard that latch click my stomach lurched and I felt a stab of heat through my groin.

I was wrong about you wanting to undress me. We were in too much of a hurry for that. In fact we didn't even make it over to the bed. I do remember you reaching up my skirt as we kissed, pulling down my underwear as I unzipped your pants.

I can only hope that no one was walking in the hallway past my room as we made love against the door, your body thrusting against mine hard and quick and fast and loud. I'm surprised the door didn't break off its hinges and fall out into the hallway, the two of us landing with it.

It's funny how with sex like that, the more fulfilling it is the more you want. It's like digging into a carton of Ben & Jerry's Chunkee Monkee. The first bite is so good, so rich and creamy and satisfying, that all you can do is keep taking bigger and bigger spoonfuls, faster and faster.

I'll never have enough of you, Max.

Bev

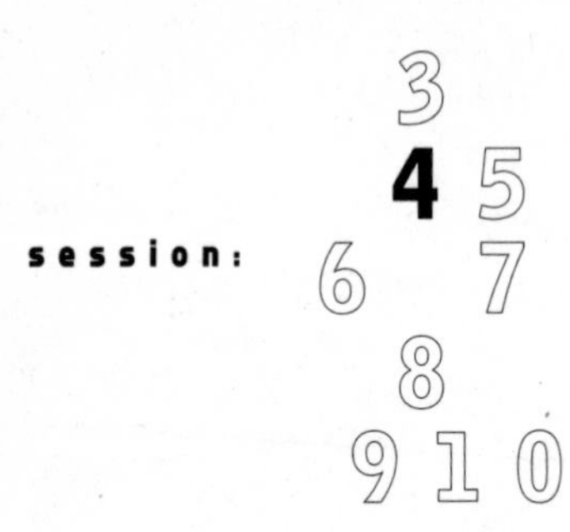

> Private Mail
> Date: Saturday, August 24, 1996 9:57 a.m.
> From: Maximilian@miller&morris.com
> Subj: In a haste I want to taste
> To: BevJ@frederic_gerard.com

Today I woke
and thoughts of you
were drawn across my eyes.
The darkness held
The vision swelled
Your face

Your breasts
Your thighs.
I longed to feel
what I could see
The warmth of rose-soft skin.
The setting stirred
The vision blurred
But the love remained within.

session: 1 2 3 4 **5** 6 7 8

> Private Mail
> Date: Sunday, August 25, 1996 7:33 p.m.
> From: Maximilian@miller&morris.com
> Subj: your poetry
> To: BevJ@frederic_gerard.com

Bev,

I hope you liked my poem. I certainly like yours.

Max

> Private Mail
> Date: Monday, August 26, 1996 6:19 a.m.
> From: BevJ@frederic_gerard.com
> Subj: my poetry?
> To: Maximilian@miller&morris.com

Max,

I didn't write you a poem.

Bev

> Private Mail
> Date: Monday, August 26, 1996 9:49 a.m.
> From: Maximilian@miller&morris.com
> Subj: yes, your poetry
> To: BevJ@frederic_gerard.com

Yes you did.

> Private Mail
> Date: Monday, August 26, 1996 12:02 p.m.
> From: BevJ@frederic_gerard.com
> Subj: no way
> To: Maximilian@miller&morris.com

No I didn't. You must be confusing me with someone else.

> Private Mail
> Date: Monday, August 26, 1996 3:26 p.m.
> From: Maximilian@miller&morris.com
> Subj: yeah way
> To: BevJ@frederic_gerard.com

I'm not confusing you with anyone else, Bev. I'm talking about the description you wrote of our night together.

> Private Mail
> Date: Monday, August 26, 1996 5:01 p.m.
> From: BevJ@frederic_gerard.com
> Subj: Oh.
> To: Maximilian@miller&morris.com

That was more like a short story, wouldn't you say?

> Private Mail
> Date: Monday, August 26, 1996 10:37 p.m.
> From: Maximilian@miller&morris.com
> Subj: Ah.
> To: BevJ@frederic_gerard.com

Whatever. I liked it.

A lot.

Will you write me another one?

Max

> Private Mail
> Date: Tuesday, August 27, 1996 8:16 a.m.
> From: BevJ@frederic_gerard.com
> Subj: Taking turns
> To: Maximilian@miller&morris.com

I think it's your turn next.

Bev

> Private Mail
> Date: Tuesday, August 27, 1996 11:55 a.m.
> From: Maximilian@miller&morris.com
> Subj: Taking turns
> To: BevJ@frederic_gerard.com

But I just wrote you that poem.

> Private Mail
> Date: Tuesday, August 27, 1996 2:47 p.m.
> From: BevJ@frederic_gerard.com
> Subj: Share and share alike
> To: Maximilian@miller&morris.com

I want more, Max. More details.

I want it all, and I want it now.

:-)

> Private Mail
> Date: Tuesday, August 27, 1996 4:35 p.m.
> From: Maximilian@miller&morris.com
> Subj: Share and share alike
> To: BevJ@frederic_gerard.com

Pretty demanding there, aren't you, little lady?

Are you this hard on your writers, too?

> Private Mail
> Date: Wednesday, August 28, 1996 5:19 a.m.
> From: BevJ@frederic_gerard.com
> Subj: Get with the program
> To: Maximilian@miller&morris.com

I'm worse. Much worse.

With you, I'm a pussycat.

Now when will I get what I want from you?

Bev

> Private Mail
> Date: Wednesday, August 28, 1996 8:27 a.m.
> From: Maximilian@miller&morris.com
> Subj: Get with the program
> To: BevJ@frederic_gerard.com

I'm working on it.

> Private Mail
> Date: Wednesday, August 28, 1996 11:46 a.m.
> From: BevJ@frederic_gerard.com
> Subj: Get with the program
> To: Maximilian@miller&morris.com

I'm waiting.

session:

6

1
2 3
4
7 8
9 1

> Thursday, August 29, 1996, 7:04 p.m.

> Writer's Forum > Live Conference > People Here: 23

DonA(Mod): Hello everyone, and thanks for joining tonight's live conference here on the Writer's Forum. For those of you who've just joined us, the topic of tonight's CO is copyright: what it is and how to protect it. Beverly Johnson, editor in chief at Frederic

Gerard Publishing and a regular contributor to the Writer's Forum, is our conference guest. Before we get started I'd like to ask everyone to try to stay on topic as much as possible, as we've got quite a lot of ground to cover and time is limited.
Beverly, thanks for joining us again. Many writers are understandably concerned about copyrights and protecting their ideas. Can you tell us how one actually goes about copyrighting an idea?

BevJ: Thanks for inviting me to return as a conference guest, Don. First, I'd like to address the common misconception that ideas can be copyrighted. They can't. It's only the creative expression of an idea into tangible form—a novel, a musical recording, a screenplay, a painting, a poem, a sculpture, for example—that can be copyrighted. In other words, you might have an idea for what you think will be the next Great American Novel, but you can't claim copyright ownership until you've actually begun writing the manuscript, expressing the idea in some sort of tangible form.

Janet: ?

DonA(Mod): GA, Janet.

Janet: Beverly, what exactly does "tangible form" mean?

DonA(Mod): Good question, Janet. GA, Bev.

BevJ: Hi Janet. Tangible form is any fixed medium such as a typewritten manuscript, a word-processing document contained on a floppy disk or any electronic file that resides on the hard drive of a computer, television and radio broadcasts, video and audio recordings, even an original drawing sketched on a cocktail napkin or a poem scribbled on notebook paper. All of these are fixed, tangible forms of expression protected by copyright law.

Janet: A lot of people think anything posted on the Internet is not protected by copyright law. Is that true? Is it because the Internet is not a tangible, fixed medium?

BevJ: Contrary to popular belief, Janet, the Internet *is* a tangible, fixed medium, and any original, creative work not in the public domain posted on the Internet or the World Wide Web *is* protected under copyright law. Thanks for asking this question, because I think it's an especially important issue these days. If you're ever tempted to download an image from the Web or reprint or redistribute an article you found on the Internet, it's best to assume that the work is copyrighted and to ask the author's permission to reproduce the item in question.

Carolyn: ?

DonA(Mod): GA, Carolyn.

Carolyn: Bev—jumping back a little bit here—I'm not sure I understand the difference between an idea and the expression of an idea. How can you copyright one and not the other?

BevJ: Another excellent question. The concept is often difficult to understand at first. Let's take a step back and look at the origin of copyright law. Our Founding Fathers included a copyright clause in the U.S. Constitution, which gives authors and other creative artists the right to own their artistic creations exclusively for a specified period of time. The idea behind this clause is to encourage the creation of new creative works and therefore promote the spread of knowledge, the arts, and human development. So let's say you have an idea to write a mystery in which someone is brutally murdered in the city of Chicago with the crime being solved by a hard-boiled female detective. You don't own the copyright to that general plot idea, but you do own the copyright to the way you've told your story via your manuscript—your particular choice of words, and the order in which your words appear—in other words, the creative selection and arrangement of the material. Another writer would be free to write a novel using this same basic plot—as long as he or she used substantially different words to tell the story—without infringing on your copyright. Or let's say you're a painter and you had an idea to paint a picture of a barn in the middle of a cornfield. Another artist could also paint a picture of a barn in a cornfield without infringing on your copyright. The two pictures would undoubtedly look completely different once they were expressed in tangible form, due to the different ways in which each of the two artists would creatively select and arrange their choice of colors, subject, and media (oils, watercolors, or pastels, for example). The idea behind this separation of an idea and the expression of an idea is to prevent a bunch of basic ideas from being tied up under copyright law, to the detriment of other creative works being contributed to the arts.

Lisa: ?

DonA(Mod): GA, Lisa.

Lisa: Hi Beverly. Does a manuscript have to be published in order to be protected by copyright law? You have to register your copyright in order for it to be protected, right?

BevJ: Hi Lisa. First, your manuscript is protected by copyright law the moment you put pen to paper or you start typing words on your computer. Furthermore, you do not have to register your copyright with the U.S. Copyright Office in order for the work to be copyrighted. Nowadays you don't even have to put a copyright notice on your published work in order for it to be copyrighted. However, it's a good idea to both put a standard copyright notice (Copyright © year and your name here) on everything you write as well as to take the additional step of registering your work with the Copyright office. By formally registering your copyright, you will be afforded certain additional legal protections such as the ability to collect damages from infringers. I should note for the benefit of lurkers here that IANAL; I don't even play one on TV. If you need legal advice you should contact a lawyer familiar with intellectual property issues.

Maximilian: <chuckle> Mustn't forget to cover our butts, right Bev?

BevJ: Hi Max. Like I said, my advice is free, so you should take it FWIW. ;-)

Maximilian: Bev, I had this idea for a screenplay, about a young woman who has a ménage à trois with two masked men...do you think I could get a copyright on it?

BevJ: Well, as I was saying earlier, Max, you'd have to actually write the screenplay first before you could copyright it. But in your case, it's important to note that a work merely has to be originally created by its author, not necessarily of a certain aesthetic quality, in order for it to be protected by copyright, so anything you wrote could probably still be covered under copyright law. <g>

Maximilian: LOL. Touché. <g>

BevJ: Seriously, Max, if your two masked men had any resemblance to, er, let's say, oh, I dunno...Batman and Robin for instance, I think you'd want to talk with Warner Brothers first, before going any further with this fascinating idea of yours. ;-)

Ian: ?

DonA(Mod): Bev, we've got a few more questions from the peanut gallery here. GA, Ian.

Ian: Hello Beverly. I'm an English teacher who's been writing fiction in my spare time for many years. My question is, do copyrights last forever, and if not, how long do they last?

BevJ: Hi Ian. No, copyrights do not last forever. For creative works published after 1977, the copyright lasts for the life of the creator plus 50 years. Copyrights can be renewed, and they can also be transferred. For example, as a writer, you may want to transfer certain rights in your copyrighted work in order to exploit the work (i.e., make money from it). So if you wanted to see your manuscript published in hardcover, you might transfer the hardcover rights to the work to a publisher. The unique thing about a copyright transfer (as opposed to other types of property transfer) is that authors or their heirs have the right to terminate any transfer of copyright ownership 35 years after it is made. So even though you are transferring specific rights to a publisher when you sign a publishing contract, it's advisable to maintain the copyright in your name, no matter what rights you are assigning in the contract.

Emmett: ?

DonA(Mod): OK Bev, I think we can take one more question. GA, Emmett.

Emmett: Bev, I'm a first-year law student, and although we haven't studied copyright law in any of my classes yet, I've found the discussion here tonight really interesting. I was wondering, aside from ideas, is there anything else that can't be copyrighted?

BevJ: As a matter of fact, Emmett, there are several things other than ideas that cannot be copyrighted. Facts, for instance, cannot be copyrighted. This includes biographical information, current events and other news, and scientific and historical facts. Let's say that, as a writer and in the course of your extensive research for a novel, you've uncovered some interesting or little-known facts. You cannot copyright these facts even though you may have spent a considerable amount of time and effort uncovering them. Of course if the facts are described in a unique way, you can copyright the expression of those facts, but not the facts themselves. In addition to facts and ideas, other things that are not protected by copyright are works published more than 75 years ago and works for which no copyright ever existed, such as anything printed by the U.S. government. All of the above material is considered public domain and can be used freely by anyone without permission.

Emmett: That's quite informative, Bev. Thank you. :-)

BevJ: You're welcome, Emmett.

DonA(Mod): I'm sorry but we've run out of time for further questions, folks. Before I send everyone off into the ether, I'd like to thank Beverly Johnson of Frederic Gerard Publishing for joining us here tonight. Bev, if any of our forum members wish to learn more about copyrights, do you have any suggestions for further resources?

BevJ: Sure, Don. The U.S. government offers a Web site that includes helpful information about copyrights as well as links to other copyright resources on the Web. That URL is http://lcweb.loc.gov/copyright. Also, Nolo Press, a publisher of legal books, publishes a book called The Copyright Handbook: How To Protect and Use Written Works, by Stephen Fishman. Nolo Press has a Web site at http://www.nolo.com. Hope this helps! Thanks everyone!

Emmett: Thanks Bev!

Janet: Bye Beverly!

%System%: DonA(Mod) has left the forum.

> 8:09 p.m.

> Writer's Forum > Live Conference > People Here: 2

Maximilian: Bev, before you go, wanna join me in a private chat room? I'm really interested in learning more about copyright issues. }:-)

BevJ: Cute. }:-)
But I can't, Max. I've got a deadline in the morning and I'm going to be up all night editing a manuscript that is currently a complete mess. How about tomorrow night? We could set a time to meet for a private chat after work sometime...

Maximilian: Er, I can't tomorrow night, Bev. I'm going to be away on a trip.

BevJ: Oh, a business trip?

Maximilian: Um, no. Steffee and I are leaving for Rehoboth Beach for a four-day weekend.

BevJ: Oh. I see.

Maximilian: I'm sorry, Bev. We've had this trip scheduled for months. I'd like nothing more than to cancel the thing entirely.

BevJ: Then why don't you?

Maximilian: Aw, Bev. Can we talk more about this another time?

BevJ: OK.

Maximilian: Thanks, Bev. I'll send you an e-mail before I go.

BevJ: Fine. Good night, Max.
Maximilian: Good night, Bev. I...

%System%: BevJ has left the forum.
%System%: Maximilian has left the forum.

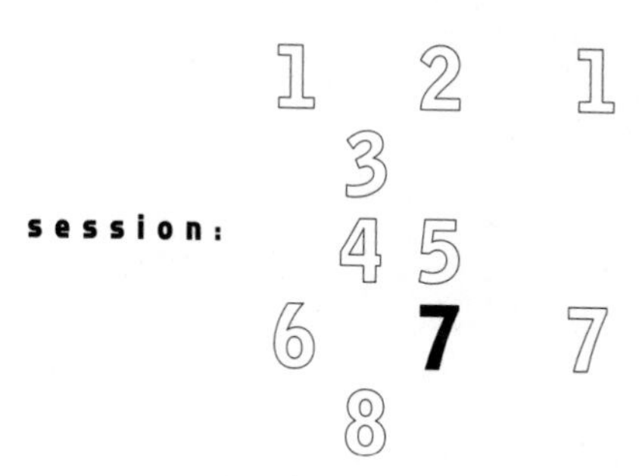

> Private Mail
> Date: Friday, August 30, 1996 1:28 a.m.
> From: Maximilian@miller&morris.com
> Subj: Nice Job
> To: BevJ@frederic_gerard.com

Bev, just a quick note before I go to sleep to let you know that I thought you did a great job at tonight's conference.

Love,

Max

> Private Mail
> Date: Friday, August 30, 1996 5:13 a.m.
> From: BevJ@frederic_gerard.com
> Subj: Blow Job
> To: Maximilian@miller&morris.com

Max,

So why don't you cancel your trip with Steffee?

Bev.

> Private Mail
> Date: Friday, August 30, 1996 7:42 a.m.
> From: Maximilian@miller&morris.com
> Subj: Schmoe Job
> To: BevJ@frederic_gerard.com

Bev,

I've thought about it, believe me.

Max

> Private Mail
> Date: Friday, August 30, 1996 8:03 a.m.
> From: BevJ@frederic_gerard.com
> Subj: Snow Job
> To: Maximilian@miller&morris.com

And?

> Private Mail
> Date: Friday, August 30, 1996 8:48 a.m.
> From: Maximilian@miller&morris.com
> Subj: Low Job
> To: BevJ@frederic_gerard.com

Pardon the pun, but your subject headers are low blows, Bev.

I find it slightly hard to be sympathetic to your jealousy when *you're* the one who's married.

> Private Mail
> Date: Friday, August 30, 1996 9:26 a.m.
> From: BevJ@frederic_gerard.com
> Subj: Foe Job
> To: Maximilian@miller&morris.com

Who said I was jealous?

And anyway, you're the one who's going off on the little lovers' getaway, not me.

> Private Mail
> Date: Friday, August 30, 1996 11:00 a.m.
> From: Maximilian@miller&morris.com
> Subj: Time To Go Job
> To: BevJ@frederic_gerard.com

Bev,

I've got to leave work in a few minutes. I know you're bothered by this. I'm bothered by it too. Just let me get through this Labor Day weekend and I promise we can talk more about this. I can't stand it when you're mad at me, Bev. Please just send me one more message before I leave and promise me you'll talk to me when I get back.

Love,

Max

> Private Mail
> Date: Friday, August 30, 1996 11:59 a.m.
> From: BevJ@frederic_gerard.com
> Subj: Woe Job
> To: Maximilian@miller&morris.com

Well, I'm not going to send you off with a smooch on the cheek and tell you to have a good time with Steffee, Max. But I will promise to talk with you after you get back. Take your time. I'll wait to hear from you.

Oh, and Max—

I love you.

Beverly

> Private Mail
> Date: Thursday, September 5, 1996 3:45 a.m.
> From: Maximilian@miller&morris.com
> Subj: Beverly
> To: BevJ@frederic_gerard.com

A thousand, no, a million stars I see tonight. Yet a wish on every one will not bring you to me.

Maximilian

p.s. I missed you.

> Private Mail
> Date: Friday, September 6, 1996 7:33 a.m.
> From: BevJ@frederic_gerard.com
> Subj: <sigh>
> To: Maximilian@miller&morris.com

Max,

I missed you, too. After five days of not receiving any e-mail from you, I thought I was going to start having the DTs.

Bev

> Private Mail
> Date: Friday, September 6, 1996 9:58 a.m.
> From: Maximilian@miller&morris.com
> Subj: <sigh>
> To: BevJ@frederic_gerard.com

You? Lose your composure? I can hardly picture it. You're as cool as a cucumber, Bev.

But I'm glad you missed me, anyway.

Max

> Private Mail
> Date: Saturday, September 7, 1996 10:22 a.m.
> From: BevJ@frederic_gerard.com
> Subj: So...
> To: Maximilian@miller&morris.com

How was your trip?

> Private Mail
> Date: Saturday, September 7, 1996 1:49 p.m.
> From: Maximilian@miller&morris.com
> Subj: So...
> To: BevJ@frederic_gerard.com

You really wanna know?

> Private Mail
> Date: Saturday, September 7, 1996 3:15 p.m.
> From: BevJ@frederic_gerard.com
> Subj: So...
> To: Maximilian@miller&morris.com

Of course I really want to know, you idiot. Why else would I have asked?

> Private Mail
> Date: Saturday, September 7, 1996 6:12 p.m.
> From: Maximilian@miller&morris.com
> Subj: So...
> To: BevJ@frederic_gerard.com

Whoa! Down girl! I wasn't *trying* to get you all riled up there.

:::mopping brow:::

I just wanted to make sure you wanted to hear the truth.

> Private Mail
> Date: Sunday, September 8, 1996 11:14 a.m.
> From: BevJ@frederic_gerard.com
> Subj: So...
> To: Maximilian@miller&morris.com

Please don't patronize me, Max. Just tell me the fucking truth, whatever it is.

> Private Mail
> Date: Sunday, September 8, 1996 9:21 p.m.
> From: Maximilian@miller&morris.com
> Subj: cyberyou/realyou
> To: BevJ@frederic_gerard.com

It was terrible, Bev.

For the entire weekend all I could think about was you. And that message you sent me right before I left. You've never told me you loved me before, Bev. I think you've known from the beginning that I fell in love with you the first night we met last year. In fact I think I had begun to fall in love with the cyberyou before I had actually met the realyou, even though I didn't know at the time that the cyberyou *is* the realyou.

And then the weekend we were together recently... you never said the words "I love you" even though I said them to you. Twice. After the second time I told you that I loved you and you didn't say anything back I thought maybe I was being a fool and that I should just shut up and enjoy the sex. But I knew from the way you looked at me and held on to me while we were making love that you felt something for me. I just wasn't sure exactly what that something was.

But now I know. And I'm happier than ever before.

And more worried than ever before. Steffee is really pissed off with me. I could hardly look at her all weekend, let alone touch her, Bev. She knows something's wrong. I don't know what to do.

How's things between you and Gary?

> Private Mail
> Date: Sunday, September 8, 1996 11:37 p.m.
> From: BevJ@frederic_gerard.com
> Subj: cyberyou/realyou
> To: Maximilian@miller&morris.com

Max, I told you I loved you the night we originally made the plans to connect for a second time. It's just that you had already left the chat room by the time I worked up the courage to say it.

And then, the weekend we were together, I didn't say it because...I just didn't want to parrot it back to you right after you said it to me. I wanted it to have more meaning than that, Max. I wanted to say it to you on my own terms, I guess.

And, there was another reason, I think.

But to answer your question, things between Gary and me are not great. I mean, how could they be? Luckily Gary's been gone so much lately—his company has been sending him to its manufacturing plants in Singapore and Malaysia—that nothing has come to a head yet.

He seems almost as preoccupied as me these days.

> Private Mail
> Date: Monday, September 9, 1996 2:33 a.m.
> From: Maximilian@miller&morris.com
> Subj: cyberyou/realyou
> To: BevJ@frederic_gerard.com

Bev,

What? What was the other reason you didn't tell me you loved me when we were together?

Max

> Private Mail
> Date: Monday, September 9, 1996 3:17 a.m.
> From: BevJ@frederic_gerard.com
> Subj: cyberyou/realyou
> To: Maximilian@miller&morris.com

Because I felt guilty, Max. I've known for a long time that I love you, and it became even more clear to me during the weekend we spent together. But I still felt terrible about what I was doing to Gary by being with you there, and I guess I felt that if I actually said the words out loud to you it would be the final insult to Gary.

> Private Mail
> Date: Monday, September 9, 1996 4:29 a.m.
> From: Maximilian@miller&morris.com
> Subj: cyberyou/realyou
> To: BevJ@frederic_gerard.com

Don't you think Gary would be more pissed off if he knew that I nearly impaled you on the hotel room door during the first time we made love that night?

I know I would.

> Private Mail
> Date: Monday, September 9, 1996 10:01 a.m.
> From: BevJ@frederic_gerard.com
> Subj: cyberyou/realyou
> To: Maximilian@miller&morris.com

Come on, Max. This is serious.

> Private Mail
> Date: Monday, September 9, 1996 12:21 p.m.
> From: Maximilian@miller&morris.com
> Subj: cyberyou/realyou
> To: BevJ@frederic_gerard.com

I'm sorry, Bev. I know this must be much harder for you than it is for me.

I can tell by the times on your messages that you're upset. Did you really stay up all night last night?

> Private Mail
> Date: Monday, September 9, 1996 4:02 p.m.
> From: BevJ@frederic_gerard.com
> Subj: cyberyou/realyou
> To: Maximilian@miller&morris.com

Yes. I couldn't fall asleep, waiting for your next message.

session: 2 6 6 7 9 0

> Private Mail
> Date: Tuesday, September 10, 1996 2:28 a.m.
> From: Maximilian@miller&morris.com
> Subj: prince charming???
> To: BevJ@frederic_gerard.com

Sometimes I drop
such a burden on you
& wonder if I'm really
worth the pain you get
when I slap your heart
with mine

& if all would be
better if I never
touched your smile
with mine
& if it'd be easier
if you had never laughed
or cried at me
& if a frog had never
really changed into a
prince, or at least thought
he had.

session: 10

4 5
7 8
9 10
13
14

> Private Mail
> Date: Wednesday, September 11, 1996 9:29 a.m.
> From: Maximilian@miller&morris.com
> Subj: on the road again
> To: BevJ@frederic_gerard.com

Bev,

I've got to go out of town tonight—on business this time, I promise. I'll be bringing my new laptop with me, but I'm going to be pretty tied up most of the week, so I don't know if I'll get much time for e-mail. We're doing the photo shoot for next year's spring swimsuit edition of the Olivia's Boutique catalog, and since we're on a tighter advertising budget this year (so what else is new), we're going to try to cram about two weeks' worth of work into one short week. But if you want to write to me I'll still try to check my messages before going to bed every night.

I love you, my darling.

Max

> Private Mail
> Date: Wednesday, September 11, 1996 12:32 p.m.
> From: BevJ@frederic_gerard.com
> Subj: on the road again
> To: Maximilian@miller&morris.com

Max,

No problem. Both of us could probably use a little break right now. Things are kind of crazy at work for me, too. I'm trying to pry a rewrite out of one of my authors, who can't come through with the goods because he's having a bad hair day or his girlfriend is bummed, or something like that. I'm ready to get on a plane myself and stand over this guy's shoulder while he does the rewrites. The book was supposed to go to the printer in a couple of weeks but I don't think it's gonna happen, obviously.

Anyhow, I hope you have a productive trip. Don't work too hard, and don't be ogling those swim-suit models too much, either. ;-)

Love,

Bev

> Private Mail
> Date: Wednesday, September 11, 1996 7:16 p.m.
> From: Maximilian@miller&morris.com
> Subj: on the road again
> To: BevJ@frederic_gerard.com

Who me? Ogle scantily clad fashion models? Why would I do that, when I can think about you and your 100% cotton underwear, white with the little pink flowers on it?

Max

p.s. I'm at the airport now. My flight's delayed so I'm sitting in the airline's VIP lounge, drinking a martini *without* anchovy olives (the nerve of some of these airlines, not having anchovy olives on hand—think I should switch airlines?), eating free peanuts, tying up one of the only two phone jacks in here, and checking to see if I had any messages from you.

> Private Mail
> Date: Thursday, September 12, 1996 7:05 a.m.
> From: BevJ@frederic_gerard.com
> Subj: surprise
> To: Maximilian@miller&morris.com

Max,

I was thinking about that last poem you wrote to

me, the one about the frog changing into a prince, and it makes me sad.

Please don't think that by coming into my life you've placed a burden on me. You've brought me a lot of happiness, Max.

I love you, still.

Bev

p.s. So you like the white ones with the pink flowers, eh? Speaking of underwear I was thinking about the underwear you wore the second night we were together in Boston, the night we went to that seafood restaurant on the pier, ate lobster, drank margaritas, and went for that "special" walk on the pier after dark...

> Private Mail
> Date: Friday, September 13, 1996 1:58 a.m.
> From: Maximilian@miller&morris.com
> Subj: surprise
> To: BevJ@frederic_gerard.com

I'm glad to know I haven't been a burden to you. You're the first woman I've ever loved, Beverly. All I want is for you to be happy.

I love you, too.

Max

p.s. Now I think *you're* the one who's getting me confused with someone else—don't you remember? I wasn't wearing any underwear on the night we took that extra special, super-duper walk on the pier. Or maybe you're thinking of one of your other boyfriends? <g>

> Private Mail
> Date: Friday, September 13, 1996 8:04 a.m.
> From: BevJ@frederic_gerard.com
> Subj: surprise
> To: Maximilian@miller&morris.com

Max,

How could I confuse you with someone else? And how could I ever forget the little surprise you had waiting for me on the pier that night?

Bev

> Private Mail
> Date: Saturday, September 14, 1996 2:26 a.m.
> From: Maximilian@miller&morris.com
> Subj: surprise
> To: BevJ@frederic_gerard.com

Well, my brazen little hussy. I didn't actually think you would find my surprise until we got back to the hotel room that night. But I can't say I'm sorry that you made your little discovery when you did! <weg>

> Private Mail
> Date: Saturday, September 14, 1996 9:29 a.m.
> From: BevJ@frederic_gerard.com
> Subj: surprise
> To: Maximilian@miller&morris.com

You're the sexiest man alive, Max. I'll never forget the sight of you...naked underneath as I undid your button-fly jeans on the pier that night.

Reminds me of a T-shirt I had as a teenager that I bought at a flea market or somewhere like that. In bold letters on the front it read: "Warning. I Am Naked Underneath My Clothes." I used to wear it all the time. I thought it was so funny.

Anyhow. Whatever possessed you to go out sans underwear that night?

Love,

Bev

> Private Mail
> Date: Sunday, September 15, 1996 12:19 a.m.
> From: Maximilian@miller&morris.com
> Subj: surprise
> To: BevJ@frederic_gerard.com

Do you still have that T-shirt, Bev? I'd love to borrow it sometime. ;-)

I'm not sure how I got the idea to skip the underwear when we were getting dressed to go out that night. The idea just sort of came over me, and I knew you would like it.

And boy was I right. I'll never forget the look on your face, Bev. We had had another wonderfully relaxing and enjoyable meal together. It was hot out and the pitcher of margaritas went down like water.

Walking down the pier arm in arm, I've never felt so peaceful in my life. We just kept on walking, talking and laughing as we went, until we found ourselves at one end of the deserted pier. It was dark and black and a little bit cooler out there, with the waves lapping at the cement pilings underneath the pier and the lights of the restaurant in the distance.

I turned to kiss you and as we kissed I felt the backs of your fingers brush against the skin below my navel and slide inside my jeans. I was hard as the rocks below and you stopped kissing me to look into my eyes. You slowly tugged at each of the buttons on my fly, one by one, and when you saw that I wasn't wearing anything underneath, you gasped, ever so softly, and dropping down to your knees, took me in your mouth.

My God, Bev.

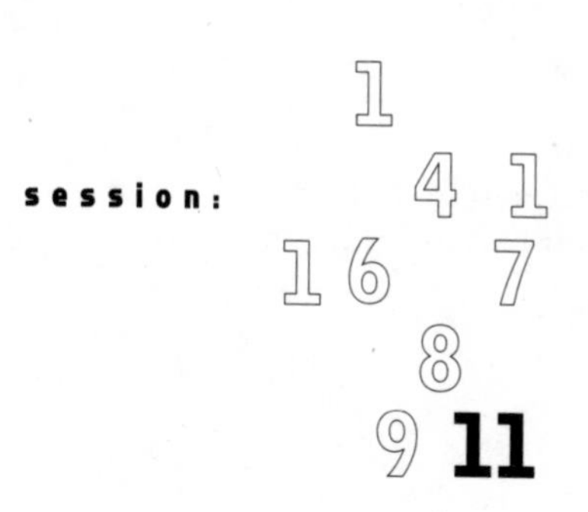

> Private Mail
> Date: Monday, September 16, 1996 6:52 a.m.
> From: BevJ@frederic_gerard.com
> Subj: He shoots he SCORES!
> To: Maximilian@miller&morris.com

Max,

I thought we were supposed to be taking a little break from each other? <g>

Whew. Well. Yes. That was a memorable evening, wasn't it?

Thank you.

Bev

p.s. I don't have that T-shirt anymore. I think I wore it so much it finally fell apart in the laundry, sort of like Seinfeld's Golden Boy.

> Private Mail
> Date: Tuesday, September 17, 1996 1:44 a.m.
> From: Maximilian@miller&morris.com
> Subj: He shoots he SCORES!
> To: BevJ@frederic_gerard.com

Hmmm. No, thank *you*.

So have you had any luck with your author who was having the bad hair day? Did he finish the rewrites for you?

And what's with the hockey reference in your

subject line? I didn't know you liked hockey (and Seinfeld—me too).

Max

> Private Mail
> Date: Tuesday, September 17, 1996 6:22 a.m.
> From: BevJ@frederic_gerard.com
> Subj: He shoots he SCORES!
> To: Maximilian@miller&morris.com

Max,

We finally got the rewrites from the bad-hair dude last night. And luckily for him they were worth the wait.

I never really liked hockey until I met you. I started watching it last winter when you wrote me that message about how you spent your Sunday afternoon watching hockey and wondering what I was doing. I still wasn't answering your messages at that time, but I thought I could at least watch the same games you were watching, as a way to be close to you without you knowing it.

And you're right, that little blue fuzzy thing they were doing with the puck on televised games is stupid.

I've always liked Seinfeld. It's one of the only TV programs I watch.

How's your photo shoot going, and when are you coming back?

Bev

> Private Mail
> Date: Tuesday, September 17, 1996 11:45 p.m.
> From: Maximilian@miller&morris.com
> Subj: You love me! You really love me!
> To: BevJ@frederic_gerard.com

God, how I wish I had known you were even reading my messages back then, Bev. But I'm glad to know I've converted you into a hockey fan. A sign of true love, I think. :-)

The photo shoot has been a nightmare. Most of the shoots are supposed to be on the beach. It rains every day here around three or four o'clock so we start at sunrise and shoot as much as we can before the rain starts. Then we pack up all of our equipment, break for a late lunch/early dinner while it's raining, come back out after the weather clears up and try to shoot more photos on the beach at sunset, usually working until nine or ten at night.

The models are exhausted, the photographer is cranky, and I miss you.

We're scheduled to fly outta here tomorrow night.

Yours Truly,

Max

> Private Mail
> Date: Thursday, September 19, 1996 7:41 a.m.
> From: BevJ@frederic_gerard.com
> Subj: Welcome Back
> To: Maximilian@miller&morris.com

Hi Max,

How was your flight last night? I hope the rest of your photo shoot went well and that you are now safely back in your apartment, snug as a bug in a rug.

xoxo,

Bev

> Private Mail
> Date: Friday, September 20, 1996 5:49 a.m.
> From: BevJ@frederic_gerard.com
> Subj: hello?
> To: Maximilian@miller&morris.com

Max? Are you there?

I haven't heard from you in a couple of days and I'm starting to get worried. When I logged online this morning I saw the News Flash about some sort of tropical storm down south and am wondering if you were affected by that.

Please write to me as soon as you get this message.

Bev

> Private Mail
> Date: Friday, September 20, 1996 7:03 a.m.
> From: Maximilian@miller&morris.com
> Subj: I'm Baaack
> To: BevJ@frederic_gerard.com

Bev,

I'm sorry if I worried you and that I wasn't able to write sooner. We were supposed to finish up the shoot on Wednesday and fly out Wednesday night, but it rained the entire day so we had to postpone our departure until last night so we could finish things up on Thursday during the day. It was frustrating because the storm knocked out a bunch of phone lines on the island and I couldn't log on to send or receive any messages. It was making me crazy, not being able to communicate with you.

Apparently the storm really screwed up the schedules for planes leaving the island, so we spent half the night at the airport because our flight kept getting delayed. What a pain in the ass. And it was such a rinky-dink little airport, there was nowhere I could plug in my laptop and modem.

I just got back to my apartment a few minutes ago and the first thing I did was fire up my computer so I could send you a message.

I'm going to bed for a few hours, and hoping I'll have dreams of you.

Good night, my love.

Max

> Private Mail
> Date: Friday, September 20, 1996 7:59 a.m.
> From: BevJ@frederic_gerard.com
> Subj: I'm Baaack
> To: Maximilian@miller&morris.com

Thank God you're OK.

I don't know what I'd do if something happened to you.

Bev

session: 1 2

3 5 5 1 7 9

> Private Mail
> Date: Friday, September 20, 1996 2:15 p.m.
> From: Maximilian@miller&morris.com
> Subj: dreams
> To: BevJ@frederic_gerard.com

Bev,

I'm back at work, staring at an unbelievably huge stack of shit that piled up on my desk while I was away. I don't even want to think about all of the interoffice e-mail I have waiting to be answered.

I can't stop thinking about you. After I got in this morning, wrote that message to you, and fell asleep, I had the strangest dream.

I was back on the beach where we were just doing the photo shoot, except in my dream you were one of the fashion models and I was the photographer. The sun was setting; the lighting was perfect; the weather was beautiful; and you looked enchanting, as always. As I photographed you, you slowly walked backward into the lush vegetation that was part of the scenery behind you, looking into the camera with that come-hither thing you do with your eyes when we're together. I kept following you and photographing you and all the while you went deeper and deeper into the vegetation until we were all the way in the jungle. Finally you stood near a bush that had these giant hibiscus flowers on it. They were the biggest flowers I had ever seen. You gently plucked one of the flowers that hadn't quite yet blossomed and slowly opened the petals of the flower while I watched. Inside the flower was a perfectly healthy, smiling baby girl.

God it was the weirdest dream, Bev. It was a good dream, but weird. It made me wonder.

After I woke up I realized that you've never told me if you and Gary have children, Bev. How stupid of me to never even ask. I know you'd make a great mom. Do you have a baby? Is that what my dream was about?

> Private Mail
> Date: Friday, September 20, 1996 5:44 p.m.
> From: BevJ@frederic_gerard.com
> Subj: dreams
> To: Maximilian@miller&morris.com

Your dream sounded lovely, Max.

But the answer is no, Gary and I don't have any children.

Bev

> Private Mail
> Date: Saturday, September 21, 1996 3:17 a.m.
> From: Maximilian@miller&morris.com
> Subj: dreams
> To: BevJ@frederic_gerard.com

Bev,

Would it be too nosy of me to ask why not? You don't have to answer if you don't want to. It's just that, like I said, I think you would make a really wonderful mother. I can't imagine you not wanting to have children.

Just tell me to shut up if I'm getting too personal.

Max

> Private Mail
> Date: Saturday, September 21, 1996 10:29 a.m.
> From: BevJ@frederic_gerard.com
> Subj: dream deferred
> To: Maximilian@miller&morris.com

It's OK, Max. The truth of the matter is that, more than anything else, I've always wanted to be a mother. But Gary and I can't have children.

> Private Mail
> Date: Saturday, September 21, 1996 2:10 p.m.
> From: Maximilian@miller&morris.com
> Subj: dream deferred
> To: BevJ@frederic_gerard.com

God do I feel like a shit.

I'm sorry I brought it up, Bev.

Can I call you? I really want to talk with you right now. I want to hear your voice and I want you to hear mine.

Max

> Private Mail
> Date: Saturday, September 21, 1996 5:20 p.m.
> From: BevJ@frederic_gerard.com
> Subj: dream deferred
> To: Maximilian@miller&morris.com

No, Max, it really wouldn't be a good idea for you to call me at home right now. Maybe you could call me at work next week, but right now wouldn't be good.

Don't feel bad about bringing it up, all right? It's OK. Really.

We tried to have children for several years. I was 31 when we got married and we started trying to conceive right away. After about a year with nothing happening, we started getting concerned, and thus began the long and expensive nightmare of endless fertility tests and procedures. The doctors could never actually figure out why we can't conceive. Neither of us was diagnosed as being infertile, and we still don't have any answers. We've given up trying for now. The tests and everything were just too stressful and the whole thing was taking over our lives in a negative sort of way. We were talking about adoption, but then...well, lately we haven't talked about it. I know it's been as hard on Gary as it has been on me, and I have to give him credit—he has never given up hope, even though I have at times.

So there you have it.

I think it's interesting that you had a dream like that about me. You must have sensed something and it surfaced in the form of a dream. It says a lot about you.

Bev

> Private Mail
> Date: Sunday, September 22, 1996 12:49 p.m.
> From: Maximilian@miller&morris.com
> Subj: dream deferred
> To: BevJ@frederic_gerard.com

I'm so sorry, Bev. I can't even imagine the pain—emotional and physical—you must have been through.

It all sort of makes sense, though. I wondered

the last time we were together why you didn't seem to use a more convenient type of birth control than a condom, being a married woman and all. <g> I thought maybe Gary had been fixed or something. I especially began to wonder near the end of our weekend together, because the last few times we made love we didn't use any protection at all.

Now I understand.

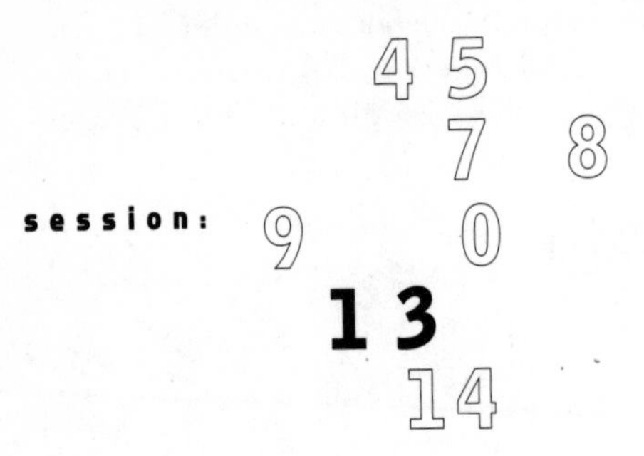

> Private Mail
> Date: Monday, September 23, 1996 10:01 a.m.
> From: Maximilian@miller&morris.com
> Subj: your voice
> To: BevJ@frederic_gerard.com

Bev,

Can I call you at work today? I just want to talk with you for a little while and hear your voice.

Max

> Private Mail
> Date: Monday, September 23, 1996 11:17 a.m.
> From: BevJ@frederic_gerard.com
> Subj: your voice
> To: Maximilian@miller&morris.com

Max,

Sure. How about around lunchtime? I was going to eat lunch at my desk today anyway. As long as you don't mind listening to me nibble on an egg salad sandwich while we chat. <g>

Bev

> Private Mail
> Date: Monday, September 23, 1996 11:48 a.m.
> From: Maximilian@miller&morris.com
> Subj: your voice
> To: BevJ@frederic_gerard.com

Great. I'm going to run down to the deli and grab a pastrami on rye. We can make it a lunch date. I'll call you at 12:15 your time.

Until then...

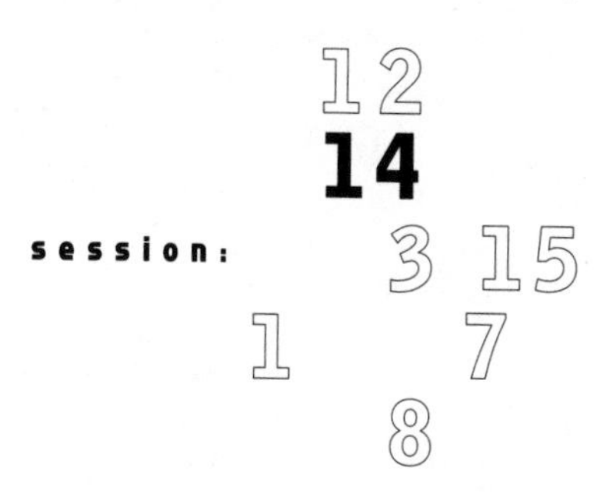

> Private Mail
> Date: Monday, September 23, 1996 2:51 p.m.
> From: Maximilian@miller&morris.com
> Subj: one question
> To: BevJ@frederic_gerard.com

God, it was great talking with you, Bev. I'm sorry I kept you on the phone so long—I didn't intend for us to talk for more than an hour. But it was really great, hearing your voice and your laughter.

I was wondering...Remember when we first met online and we played that game where you let me ask you one question, and I let you ask me one question? Could we do that again? I want to ask you a question, but I didn't have the gonads to ask you on the phone.

Love,

Max

> Private Mail
> Date: Monday, September 23, 1996 3:19 p.m.
> From: BevJ@frederic_gerard.com
> Subj: one question
> To: Maximilian@miller&morris.com

Of course, Max. I have a question I've been wanting to ask you, too.

You go first.

Love,

Bev

p.s. I enjoyed talking with you, too. You give good phone. :-)

> Private Mail
> Date: Monday, September 23, 1996 6:26 p.m.
> From: Maximilian@miller&morris.com
> Subj: one question
> To: BevJ@frederic_gerard.com

OK. I know you'll think this is a strange question, Bev, but I was wondering if you'd tell me how you and Gary met and all that.

Max

> Private Mail
> Date: Tuesday, September 24, 1996 5:17 a.m.
> From: BevJ@frederic_gerard.com
> Subj: one question
> To: Maximilian@miller&morris.com

Really?

That *is* a strange question for you to ask, Max.

Are you sure you want to know? I'm surprised you would want me to share something like that with you.

Bev

> Private Mail
> Date: Tuesday, September 24, 1996 8:45 a.m.
> From: Maximilian@miller&morris.com
> Subj: one question
> To: BevJ@frederic_gerard.com

Yes, I really want to know, Bev. I'm not sure why...I just think it will help me understand some things.

It won't change how much I love you, I promise.

Max

> Private Mail
> Date: Tuesday, September 24, 1996 7:24 p.m.
> From: BevJ@frederic_gerard.com
> Subj: one answer
> To: Maximilian@miller&morris.com

OK, Max. It feels strange talking about this with you, but I gave you my word. Here goes:

Gary and I met when I was 30, during the summer of 1989 on a miniature golf course. I was with some friends and he was in the group behind us with some of his friends. They were golfing much faster than we were, so every time I took a shot it seemed Gary was there waiting for us to finish up the hole. I'm a klutz when it comes to most sports, but for some strange reason I'm really good at pool and miniature golf. That night I got four holes in one, and Gary happened to be watching every time. At the 18th hole he said he'd buy me an ice-cream cone if I got another hole in one, and sure enough I did.

So he bought me a vanilla twist on a plain cone, and got the same for himself. We sat on the picnic bench outside the miniature golf course eating the ice cream while our friends went go-kart racing. We made the usual small talk like where do you work and where do you live and stuff like that. In the middle of our conversation Gary started scrunching up his nose and sniffing at his ice cream with a real strange look on his face. I asked him what was wrong. He said that he thought his ice cream smelled funny and asked me if I would smell it just to make sure he wasn't imagining there was something wrong with his ice cream. So I leaned over to sniff his ice-cream cone and the stinker pushed his cone up my nose, laughing his ass off and leaving me with vanilla soft-serve dripping off my nose.

I couldn't believe he did that. And yet, I thought it was funny, too, and charming in an odd sort of way. Most of the guys I had been dating at the time seemed intimidated by me, always trying to kiss my butt, and I guess I found Gary's sense of humor refreshing. We started dating and got married the following year. We were both at a point in our lives where we felt we knew what we wanted, so we didn't waste a whole lot of time with a long engagement or anything.

Is that what you wanted to know? I hope I'm not freaking you out by telling you all this, Max.

> Private Mail
> Date: Wednesday, September 25, 1996 3:07 a.m.
> From: Maximilian@miller&morris.com
> Subj: one answer
> To: BevJ@frederic_gerard.com

Thanks Bev. I'm not sure it's what I *wanted* to know. But it's what I needed to know.

I love you, still.

Good night.

> Private Mail
> Date: Wednesday, September 25, 1996 6:27 a.m.
> From: BevJ@frederic_gerard.com
> Subj: one question
> To: Maximilian@miller&morris.com

It was hard to tell you all that. It made me feel...uncomfortable.

But now, I have a question for you. Can I?

> Private Mail
> Date: Wednesday, September 25, 1996 11:28 a.m.
> From: Maximilian@miller&morris.com
> Subj: one question
> To: BevJ@frederic_gerard.com

Shoot.

> Private Mail
> Date: Wednesday, September 25, 1996 7:02 p.m.
> From: BevJ@frederic_gerard.com
> Subj: one question
> To: Maximilian@miller&morris.com

Will you marry me?

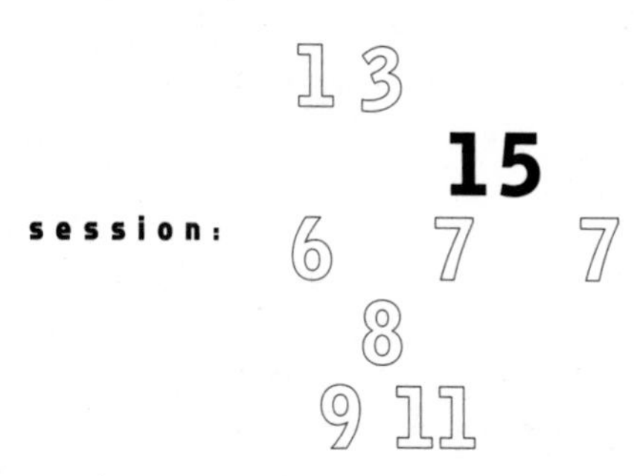

> Private Mail
> Date: Thursday, September 26, 1996 1:09 a.m.
> From: Maximilian@miller&morris.com
> Subj: holy shit!!!!!!!
> To: BevJ@frederic_gerard.com

Ohmygod Bev. You had better be serious or I swear to God I'm going to drive straight to that half-assed city of yours and pull out every one of your pretty little fingernails.

Of course yes. Yes I want to marry you. I've been

wanting to ask you myself for the longest time but I didn't want to put you on the spot. I couldn't bring myself to ask you to divorce Gary, and when you told me how you met him and all that I decided then and there I would never ask you and just try to let us keep going the way we were as long as I could.

After I came in last night and got your message I was so floored I mixed myself a double martini to calm myself down and I'm having another as I write this. I am starting to get trashed right now Bev but yes yes I'll marry you.

When and where do you think we should get married? In Vegas maybe at that Elvis cathedral or something?

I'll quit my job and you can keep yours. I hate that fuckin' place anyway and I can get another job. I already broke up with Steffee—I know I didn't tell you that but I didn't want you to feel bad about it.

Yours forever,

Max

> Private Mail
> Date: Thursday, September 26, 1996 7:16 a.m.
> From: BevJ@frederic_gerard.com
> Subj: no shit
> To: Maximilian@miller&morris.com

Max,

First of all, I hope you've stopped drinking martinis by now. <g>

And of course I'm serious. I'm serious as a heart attack. I've been fantasizing about marrying you for a long time but recently it's become more than a fantasy. It's the only thing left for us to do.

I was thinking maybe we should get together in the next couple of weeks—sort of an early birthday present for me. But most important, we could spend the weekend talking and making sure that this is something we both want and can live with.

What do you think?

Bev

p.s. And no, we are not getting married in the drive-thru Elvis chapel.

> Private Mail
> Date: Thursday, September 26, 1996 3:25 p.m.
> From: Maximilian@miller&morris.com
> Subj: splitting headache
> To: BevJ@frederic_gerard.com

Bev,

I've stopped drinking martinis but I refuse to even discuss our engagement any further until you agree to marry me in the drive-thru Elvis cathedral.

Max

> Private Mail
> Date: Thursday, September 26, 1996 8:38 p.m.
> From: BevJ@frederic_gerard.com
> Subj: Only Fools Rush In
> To: Maximilian@miller&morris.com

OK, OK. We can do the Elvis chapel thing! Whatever it takes. I just want to be with you.

Now about getting together for a weekend to talk more about this—what do you think?

Bev

> Private Mail
> Date: Friday, September 27, 1996 12:41 a.m.
> From: Maximilian@miller&morris.com
> Subj: A Fool Such As I
> To: BevJ@frederic_gerard.com

I think it's a grand idea, Bev.

How about if I fly to Chicago the weekend of your birthday? That's two weeks from today—do you think you could make arrangements to get away for a couple of nights, so we could stay together in a hotel downtown?

Max

> Private Mail
> Date: Friday, September 27, 1996 7:20 a.m.
> From: BevJ@frederic_gerard.com
> Subj: It's Now or Never
> To: Maximilian@miller&morris.com

I can arrange it. I'll make reservations at the Four Seasons for Friday and Saturday nights, the 11th and 12th.

I can't wait to see you again.

Bev

> Private Mail
> Date: Friday, September 27, 1996 10:26 a.m.
> From: Maximilian@miller&morris.com
> Subj: Can't Help Falling In Love
> To: BevJ@frederic_gerard.com

I can't wait to see you either, Bev.

I know it will be hard, but let's not contact each other during these next two weeks. I think it would give us both a chance to clear our heads a bit. Also...this is going to be a lot more complicated for you than it will be for me, Bev, and I want to give you some time to think more clearly about this without me placing any further undue influence over you with my incredibly witty and charming e-mails and phone calls. <g>

Seriously—I want to give you the chance to think about all the implications of a decision such as this, and if at any point you change your mind, Bev, all you have to do is tell me and I'll leave you alone forever.

The one thing I won't do is cancel this trip. Whether we decide to spend the rest of our lives together or not, I won't give up the chance to spend your birthday with you. It will either be our last time together before we part or the first weekend of a new beginning for both of us. But now that I know how much you love me, nothing can stop me from coming to see you.

I love you, Bev.

Max

> Private Mail
> Date: Friday, September 27, 1996 1:14 p.m.
> From: BevJ@frederic_gerard.com
> Subj: The Wonder of You
> To: Maximilian@miller&morris.com

And I love you, Max.

session: 16

> Private Mail
> Date: Friday, October 11, 1996 3:33 p.m.
> From: Maximilian@miller&morris.com
> Subj: Love You Forever
> To: BevJ@frederic_gerard.com

Beverly,

I'm sending this from the plane on my way to see you. It's been a bumpy ride so far—a double martini sounds good about now.

I wanted to tell you once more before I meet you at the hotel tonight how much I love you and how happy you've made me. Since you asked me to marry you two weeks ago, Bev, I've been walking around in a fantastic state of disbelief. You are the first thing I think of when I wake up. All day I think of nothing but you. When I go to sleep I dream of what our life together is going to be like.

I have to log off now. The pilot just asked us to shut down our electronic devices.

In a few hours I'll have you in my arms, where you belong.

Yours Forever,

M

> Friday, October 11, 1996, 4:44 p.m.

> News Flash
> Your Online Source for Today's Hottest Headlines

Top News: Plane Crashes Near Lake Michigan
NY–Chicago Flight Downed by Thunderstorms
Rescuers Search for Survivors

In Other News:
Stock Market Continues to Plunge
House Ethics Committee Convenes
Satellite Captures Photos of New Galaxy

Conferences & Chats:
Meet the Men Behind Blue Man Group
Vote: Favorite Films of All Time
Halloween Mystery Writers Contest
New Flat Rate Pricing Info

online glossary

acronyms & abbreviations

AFK	away from keyboard
AOL	America Online
BG	big grin
BPS	bits per second
BRB	be right back
BTW	by the way
CIS	CompuServe Information Service
CO	conference
CUL	see you later
CULA	see you later alligator
F2F	face-to-face
FWIW	for what it's worth
FYA	for your amusement
FYI	for your information
G	grin
GA	go ahead

GAL	get a life
G,D&R	grinning, ducking & running
G,D&RVVF	grinning, ducking & running very very fast
GMTA	great minds think alike
HTML	HyperText Markup Language
IANAD	I am not a doctor
IANAL	I am not a lawyer
IMA	I might add
IMHO	in my humble opinion
IMNSHO	in my not-so-humble opinion
IMO	in my opinion
LOL	laughing out loud
Net	short for Internet
NRN	no reply necessary
OTOH	on the other hand
PMFJI	pardon me for jumping in
ROFL	rolling on floor laughing
RSN	real soon now
TIA	thanks in advance
TIPOOTV	though I play one on TV (as in, IANAL, TIPOOTV)
TPTB	the powers that be
VBG	very big grin
Web	short for World Wide Web
WEG	wicked evil grin
WWW	World Wide Web
YMMV	your mileage may vary

emoticons & other symbols

:-)	smile
;-)	wink
:-(	frown
:-*	kiss
:'-(	crying
}:-)	horny smile
{}	hug
< > or :: ::	signifies something that the writer is doing or pretending to do, such as <sigh> or ::going to get body oil now::
>>>>	indicates that the words following this symbol are being quoted from another message
* * or _ _	indicates emphasis of the word or phrase typed inside these symbols

colophon

The typefaces used in this book are Faktos and Bell Gothic Black for the chapter heads and Adobe Caslon and Adobe Caslon Expert for the body text.

ABOUT THE AUTHOR

NAN MCCARTHY WAS BORN IN CHICAGO IN 1961 AND IS A FORMER COMPUTER JOURNALIST. CHAT, CONNECT, AND CRASH ARE NAN'S FIRST NOVELS. SHE IS CURRENTLY WORKING ON HER NEXT BOOK, A BLUES NOVEL SET IN THE SOUTH SIDE OF CHICAGO. NAN LIVES IN GRAYSLAKE, ILLINOIS, WITH HER HUSBAND, THEIR TWO SONS, ONE DOG, FIVE CATS, AND AN AMAZING GOLDFISH NAMED ELVIS. YOU CAN VISIT NAN'S WEB SITE AT HTTP://WWW.RAINWATER.COM OR WRITE TO HER AT NAN@RAINWATER.COM